Vinegar Pancakes and Vanishing Cream

Vinegar Pancakes and Vanishing Cream

BONNIE PRYOR

ILLUSTRATED BY GAIL OWENS

A YEARLING BOOK

Published by
Dell Publishing
a division of
Bantam Doubleday Dell Publishing Group, Inc.
666 Fifth Avenue
New York, New York 10103

ISBN: 0-440-40173-9

Reprinted by arrangement with William Morrow and Company, Inc.

Printed in the United States of America

June 1989

10 9 8 7 6 5 4 3

CW

TO THE ORIGINAL VINEGAR PANCAKE GANG

❧CONTENTS❧

❦ 1 ❦

HOW TO BE A TELEVISION STAR

Maybe if I were rich and famous, I wouldn't mind having a name like Martin Elwood Snodgrass. I wouldn't even mind having red hair, about a million freckles, and being the shortest kid in Mrs. Robbin's third grade.

On top of a rotten name, I got stuck with a brother who is a Little League baseball star and captain of the swim team; a sister who's so smart she got to skip first grade; and a little brother so cute people "ohh" and "ahh" over him wherever we go. My mother just became the mayor of New Albany, where we live. And my father is the most popular doctor in town. Sometimes I wonder why I even get up in the morning.

I think I will change my name when I grow up. Something like John Smith or Bill Brown would be nice. Martin Elwood Snodgrass sounds like something you would say if you shut your finger in a door and your mother was standing next to you.

I asked my Dad if he ever thought about changing our name. But he said it was a good name that went all the way back to a duke or earl or something like that. Then I asked him about changing M or at least Elwood. He said I was named M after one grandfather and Elwood after the and their feelings would be hurt if I changed one. I wonder why no one thought about ho feelings were going to be hurt with a name like

Dad said having a name like Snodgrass seemed to bother my brother Tim. Of course Who is going to call you Snotgrass if you are biggest kid in class, a terrific swimmer, and the pitcher the Little League has ever had? No would care if your name was Pumpernickel.

Actually, changing my name wouldn't do good unless I had brown hair like Mom. Everyone else in my family has red hair like mine. That means that everybody in New Albany recognizes me wherever I go. "Oh, you are one of the Snodgrass kids," grown-ups always say. Then they wonder what great things I've been up to. Even my brother Robbie, who is not quite two, and never remembers to go to the bathroom until it's too late, has had his picture in the paper and been on television. It happened on Mom's first day as mayor of New Albany.

We had a lot of babysitters while Mom was running for mayor. She had to give a lot of speeches and go to a lot of meetings. As soon as she was elected, Mom had to put an ad in the paper for a housekeeper. A lot of ladies applied for the job, but most of them left when they discovered there were four kids. Finally Mrs. Albright came. She looked like a grandmother. We all liked her right away. But she couldn't start work until Tuesday, and Mom started being mayor on Monday. Caroline, Tim, and I would all be in school, but there was no one to watch Robbie.

"Maybe you could take him to your office," Mom suggested to Dad. His office was in the back of our house.

"You don't want Robbie around all those sickies," Tim said.

"My patients are not sickies," Dad said. "But Tim is right, this is the flu season. Take him with you," Dad said soothingly to Mom. "He'll be all right in the playpen. You won't have much to do the first day anyway."

Mom left for her first morning as mayor with a cheerful smile—and Robbie. When she came home that night she handed Robbie to Dad and headed straight for the couch with a cool towel for her head. We had all forgotten how much Robbie hates the playpen. When you put him in it he screams and shakes the bars like he's in jail. I don't blame him. I'll bet I hated it when I was a baby, too, even though I don't remember now.

Mom had had to take Robbie out of the playpen. She said it wasn't too bad at first because Robbie kept busy dropping pens and erasers into the waste-paper basket. Then he found a typewriter ribbon and unwound the whole thing. Mom cleaned him up the best she could because the commissioners of parks and water invited her to lunch. They went to the Golden Spoon, the fanciest restaurant in town. Robbie wanted a peanut butter sandwich and wouldn't eat anything else. But they didn't have any peanut butter. I guess peanut butter isn't fancy enough.

The waitress brought Robbie some Jell-O all cut up in little squares. That's another thing about fancy restaurants. They don't know that kids hate green Jell-O, even if it is in squares. While Mom was talking to the commissioner of parks, Robbie was throwing the green squares at the head of the water department. It's too bad they didn't bring Robbie some red gelatin. He would have eaten that.

Mom said the man was pretty nice about it, considering the green didn't look very good on his white shirt. Even so, she decided she would take the rest of the day off and take Robbie home. But when she called her office, her secretary said the newspaper was sending someone to take her picture, so Mom went back to work.

The newspaper reporter arrived, and so did some reporters from the local television station. They said they had heard about Robbie and thought it would make a nice story for the evening news.

The newspaper wanted a picture of Mom signing her first proclamation as mayor. But no one could find the paper until one of the television crew noticed Robbie chewing on something.

It was all in the paper that night, and on the six o'clock news. There was Robbie chewing on the proclamation, his face smeared with green Jell-O and blue ink.

Dad held Robbie while we listened to Mom's story. "Well, young man," Dad said sternly, "it sounds like you were very busy today."

"Robbie work," he said proudly.

"Did you do anything else?" Dad asked.

My famous little brother thought about that for a while, then he nodded. "Robbie wet pants," he said happily.

❧ 2 ❧

FRECKLES ARE FOREVER

One day at school my teacher, Mrs. Robbin, told us that the body is always shedding cells and growing new ones.

"Mom," I asked that night, "Dad's a pretty good doctor, isn't he?"

"Your father is the best doctor in the world," Mom said.

"Couldn't he put me to sleep, like when I had my tonsils out, and scrape off my freckles?"

Mom gave me one of her looks. "Of course not! It would hurt. And it wouldn't work. Besides," she said, kissing my cheek, "they look cute."

"Cute" is pretty far down on the list of things I

want to be. But it's pretty hard to explain that to a mother. It was then that I first noticed the v-a-n-i-s-h-i-n-g cream on Mom's dresser.

"What's this?" I asked.

"Vanishing cream," said Mom.

"Do you use it for magic tricks?" I asked.

Mom smiled. "Something like that. I use it to get rid of age spots."

"You get spots when you get old?"

Mom showed me a little spot on her hand. "Like this. The cream fades it away, and makes my hand prettier."

Now I knew why Mom didn't have freckles like the rest of us. She might call it an age spot, but she couldn't fool me. That spot was a freckle. I thought about it all that night. The next morning was the beginning of winter break. When Mom went to work, I decided to try the cream. I put a big glob on my face and rubbed it in.

I wasn't sure how long I should leave it on. Fifteen minutes ought to be enough. Any more than that and Mrs. Albright, our housekeeper, might see me when she came upstairs to make my parents' bed. Or even worse, my sister, Caroline, might find out. Caroline is the world's biggest tattletale.

I was just sitting there, watching the clock, when in walked Caroline.

"I'm going to tell," she said gleefully.

"Don't you dare." I made the meanest face I could with all that cream smeared on it.

"What will you give me if I don't?"

I sighed. "What do you want?"

"This is my week to dry dishes. You do them for me, and I won't tell."

"All week?"

"Every day." Caroline smirked.

"All right," I agreed.

I looked in the mirror when I wiped off the cream. As far as I could see, not one freckle had vanished. But maybe you had to use it a few times. Since I didn't have to worry about Caroline telling anymore, I tried it again the next day.

Caroline appeared in the doorway. "This time I'm *really* going to tell."

"You can't. We made a bargain. And I dried your stupid dishes last night," I said.

"That bargain was for yesterday. This is a new day."

"What do you want this time?" I groaned.

"Let's see," Caroline said slowly. "I know. The next time my friend Mandy comes over and we play house, you have to be the baby."

"No. I won't do it." I shook my head and little globs of cream fell on the dresser.

Caroline shrugged. "Suit yourself. Better be ready to be in big trouble tonight."

"Okay," I yelled. "But that means you don't tell for the rest of the week."

Every morning I sat with cream on my face. Every night I dried dishes. In between I prayed that Mandy would get some contagious disease so she couldn't come over—at least until I could get something on Caroline. By Saturday I was ready to give up. Actually, I didn't have any choice. The cream was almost gone. I hoped Mom would think that Robbie got into it. Robbie gets into everything.

"Martin," Mom said that night, "have you been using my vanishing cream?"

I hung my head. "I didn't mean to use it all."

Mom looked at me for a long time. "Freckles?" she asked.

I nodded again. "It didn't make any of them vanish."

"I think your freckles are very handsome," Mom said.

"You wouldn't think so if the kids called you stuff like Snotgrass."

Mom said the kids were only teasing, and I should try to ignore them. She said I should learn to accept myself. I wasn't really listening. All I could think of was that I had dried the dishes all week for nothing. Mom wasn't even very mad. I still had every freckle and now it was *my* turn to dry dishes.

The only good thing was that I didn't have to play house with Caroline and Mandy.

3

TOO DUMB TO CATCH

My brother Tim has a whole row of trophies on his bedroom shelf. There are trophies for baseball and swimming and even one for bowling. At the rate he is winning them, soon we will have to have a special room just for his trophies. It will have a big sign on the door saying "Trophy Room," and Mrs. Albright will go in once a week to dust and polish everything. Dad will take visitors through the room, and they will say things like "Wow" and "Amazing." Then maybe the visitors will see me hanging around and want to see my trophies. I'll have to show them the only one I have. Caroline gave it to me for my birthday last year. It's made of plastic and says "World's Greatest Pest" in gold letters on the front.

Sometimes Tim tries to teach me things. "Why don't you come to the pool," he said one day. "If you'd learn how to swim, you could be on my team."

That would be nice. Maybe I could win some trophies, too. But there is a small problem. Whenever I get in the water, I sink.

"You just have to use positive thinking," Tim said when I told him. "Think about all those battleships and oil tankers. They weigh tons more than you do, and they float."

"A battleship doesn't have to worry about getting his face in the water," I said.

"You get your face wet when you wash it, don't you?" Tim asked.

"Sure I do. But I never heard of anyone drowning in the bathroom sink."

"All right. So you don't like to swim. How about baseball then? They play that on dry land."

"I'm not very good at catching," I said.

"Neither was I when I first started," Tim said generously. "At least I don't think I was. I really don't remember being as clumsy as you, but I must have been before I learned. I'll tell you what. I haven't got anything to do right now. I'll give you a few pointers."

"I don't think I can," I said.

"I told you. You have to think you can. I'm going to let you use my new catcher's mitt. Even *you* could catch with it."

"Do you really think so?"

"Sure. It's a great mitt." He went up to his room to get it, and a few minutes later we were out in the yard ready to start.

"I'll just throw a few easy ones at first," Tim said.

The mitt did feel good on my hand. Tim was right, I told myself. Anyone could catch with a mitt like this. It even smelled good, which is a lot more than I can say for Tim after he's played a game.

"Ready?"

I nodded and Tim threw the ball. I saw a blur whizzing toward me and stepped out of the way. The ball sailed by.

"Why didn't you catch it?" Tim shouted.

"I thought it was going to hit me."

"You are supposed to catch it so it doesn't hit you," Tim said. "I'm throwing it as easy as I can."

"Maybe I just wasn't ready."

"Okay, we'll try it again. Here it comes," Tim said.

The ball was coming right at me again. I had to duck. I couldn't stop myself. Wouldn't anybody duck with something coming at them at nine hundred miles an hour?

"You did it again," Tim yelled.

"I couldn't help it."

"I've got an idea," Tim said. "Put your feet in one spot. Don't move them, no matter what."

"I won't move my feet," I promised.

This time the ball flew over my head. I didn't really see it because my eyes were closed. I didn't want to see the ball come crashing into me. I did reach up for it when I heard it whizz by, but I missed. Tim was pretty nice about it. He didn't yell, or call me a dummy. He sat down on the grass and was very quiet.

"Why didn't you jump for the ball?" Tim asked after a few minutes.

"You told me not to move my feet," I said.

"I knew you were going to say that." Tim sighed. "How about football? Do you like that?"

I shook my head. "Soccer?" he asked. "I've got it. Tennis. Tennis balls are really soft."

"I guess I don't really like any kind of sports," I told him.

Tim looked like a nine-hundred-mile-an-hour

ball had hit him in the face. "You don't like any sports?" he croaked.

"Well, I like to watch you play," I said, giving him back the mitt.

I could see that made him feel a little better. "I can't decide if I want to swim in the Olympics, or play major-league baseball when I grow up," he said. "Or maybe I'll try football. What do you want to do?" he asked.

"I don't know yet."

"Well, you'd better figure it out pretty soon," he said. "Maybe you could do something really fantastic. Like Thomas Edison," he said, patting me on the shoulder. "He invented the light bulb, so no one knows if he was good at sports or not. If you could invent something to make you really famous like that, no one would ever know you are too dumb to catch a ball."

4

ORDINARY BOY HERO

I never thought much about my name or how I looked until a few days after I started third grade.

Mrs. Robbin had us line up in alphabetical order to go to the gym. The boy in front of me was Willie Smith. I had already noticed Willie because he was the biggest kid in class. Willie knew all about third grade. It was his second time there.

Willie turned around in line. "What's your name, carrot head?" he asked, looking down at me. He was a whole head taller.

"Martin Snodgrass," I answered innocently.

"Martin Snodgrass?" Willie burst out laughing.

"Hey, David," he yelled to another boy, "he says his name is Snotgrass. He blows his nose on the grass."

By lunchtime everyone was calling me Snotgrass. I was so miserable I wanted to run home and lock myself in my room for the rest of my life. But I knew Mom and Dad would never let me quit school in the third grade. For the next few days I didn't talk to anyone.

Then one afternoon I was watching some boys playing catch on the playground, and one of the boys missed the ball. If I caught it and made a good throw, maybe they would ask me to play. Maybe they would stop snickering every time I walked past. I made a flying leap for the ball.

"I've got it," I yelled. But I forgot I'd been sitting with my feet wrapped around the legs of a bench. I landed flat on my face in the dirt. I skinned my knee and nose. The ball went sailing by, and everyone laughed as I picked myself up.

Even if my feet had not been tangled I probably would have missed the ball. No matter how I tried I could never be like Tim.

"That boy was born with a ball in his hands," someone told Dad one day when we'd gone to see Tim pitch a no-hitter.

Dad grinned proudly. "I guess he's a chip off the old block. I played a little ball myself when I was in college."

I figure Dad will never call me a chip off the old block. What he says to me is, "Martin, you are not even trying."

What's the use of trying? Whatever I do, someone in my family can do better. Sports, smarts, looks—it's all covered.

It's the same at school. "Martin, why don't you have Caroline help you with your reading?" Mrs. Robbin suggested. "She was a wonderful reader when she was in my room."

What I need is to do something no one in the family can do. Something to make me famous. Like being a hero. But even though I've watched for a chance very carefully, hoping to find somebody to save, no one ever gets in trouble when I'm around. I don't know where the heroes on television find people to help. Maybe they live in more exciting towns than New Albany.

Jamie Jamison is my only friend at school. He's the only one who's never made fun of my name. One day while we were eating lunch, he gave me an idea.

"My cat Muff is going to have kittens," he said,

picking the lettuce out of his tuna fish sandwich. "Would you like one when they are born?"

I shook my head. "My parents don't want any pets," I started to say when—boing! It was just like in the comic books. A light bulb went on over my head.

One time I had seen a picture of a fire fighter rescuing a cat from a tree. This would be even better. I could just picture the headlines: "ORDINARY BOY RESCUES MOTHER-TO-BE." "Ordinary boy hero" sounded even better. Unfortunately, Jamie didn't think much of my idea.

"Muff doesn't need rescuing," he said. "She climbs trees all the time."

"But she is going to be a mother. She shouldn't be climbing up and down trees all the time. It might not be good for her."

Jamie looked thoughtful. "Maybe you're right. But wait a minute. How are we going to get her up in the tree right when you want to save her?"

I thought for a minute. "We could pretend we are dogs and bark at her. Come on, Jamie. I thought we were friends."

"We are." Jamie frowned. "All right. I'll help you. But first I want to be sure you can climb high enough to save her."

"Of course I can. I climb trees at home all the time." That much was true. But I didn't mention that I never climbed very high. Going higher couldn't be too hard. You just keep on climbing—and try not to look down.

❧ 5 ❧

WHAT GOES UP MUST COME DOWN

Mom agreed to let me go home with Jamie after school. "I'll pick you up when I come home from work," she said.

It took me a long time to decide what to wear that day. I wanted to look my best if I was going to have my picture in the paper. I almost wore my T-shirt that said "Super Hero" on it, but at the last minute I changed my mind. Heroes have to be humble and say things like, "It was nothing" or "I was only doing my job." I put on my new plaid shirt and almost-new jeans. Mom raised an eyebrow when I came to breakfast. I don't usually like to dress up. But she believed me when I said I wanted Jamie's mother to like me.

Jamie's mother was a round lady with curly hair. "Come and have some cookies and milk," she said when we walked in. Mom and Dad only allow us to have fruit after school so we don't spoil our supper. I didn't want to hurt her feelings, so I ate four gooey chocolate chip cookies, but I said "No, thank you" very politely when she offered me a fifth.

"Oh, your mother is the mayor, isn't she?" Mrs. Jamison smiled. "I saw your little brother on TV. He was so cute. Have you ever been on TV, Martin?"

"Not yet," I mumbled.

"What's that?" Mrs. Jamison asked.

"We're going to go outside and play, Mom," Jamie said quickly. Muff, the cat, was sitting on top of the refrigerator, purring loudly. Mrs. Jamison saw me looking at her and laughed.

"Cats go where they want to go. We've tried and tried to teach her to stay off there, but she likes the warmth of the motor. I just hope she doesn't decide to have her family up there."

Jamie led me to a tall maple tree in the front yard. "This is the one she usually climbs."

"Okay." I nodded, looking up at the tree. It looked awfully high. "I'll climb it once to show you I can do it. Then we'll chase the cat up into it. When I start up after her you run in and tell your

Mom. Tell her she had better call the paper. They'll want a picture for the front page."

I started up the tree. It wasn't too hard at first.

"You'll have to go higher than that," Jamie called. "Muff always goes way up to the top."

The branches were getting thinner and closer together. Little twigs scratched my face. I climbed higher. I was beginning to get a sinking feeling in the pit of my stomach. The wind was blowing just hard enough to make the branches sway back and forth.

"Don't forget," Jamie shouted—his voice was beginning to sound far away—"you'll have to climb down with only one hand because you will be holding the cat."

That's when I made my mistake. I looked down. Suddenly the ground seemed to be moving. I twisted my foot to get a firmer hold, and *snap*, the branch broke! I grabbed for the trunk as I felt myself sliding through the branches. One of them caught on my new shirt and I heard a rip. This is it, I thought. I'm going to die. They will probably have a nice funeral. I could see everyone crying. "He was a pretty good kid," Dad would say. "I wish I'd called him a chip off the old block." Willie would be there. "I really thought Snodgrass was a

wonderful name," he would sob. And Mrs. Robbin would say, "He was such a lovely child. Who cares if he couldn't read as well as Caroline?"

Suddenly I realized that I wasn't moving. Somehow my legs had caught on another branch halfway down. There I was, hanging upside down by my knees.

"What are you doing?" Jamie yelled.

I thought quickly. "Pretty neat trick, huh? Bet you couldn't do that."

"You did that on purpose?" Jamie sounded suspicious.

"Of course," I said, trying to keep my voice from shaking. "I do stuff like this all the time at home." I pulled myself up and climbed the rest of the way down.

"I think you fell," Jamie said when I reached the bottom. "You scratched your face."

"Well, the branch broke," I admitted.

"You better not do that when you're rescuing Muff," Jamie said.

I tried not to limp as we went into the house for the cat. Jamie's mother was upstairs. We got the kitchen stool and grabbed the cat off the refrigerator. Muff snuggled in Jamie's arms and purred.

"I feel kind of mean," Jamie said.

"We won't hurt her," I promised. "We'll just bark enough to make her climb part way up. High enough to make it look real. Then when I climb after her, you have your Mom call the paper. Tell them to come fast because I don't want to have to stay up in the tree all night."

We sat Muff down by the tree. "Woof, woof," we barked loudly. Muff looked at us for a second. Then she started giving herself a bath.

"Maybe she's not afraid of dogs," I said.

We howled, growled, and jumped up and down waving our arms. Finally Muff decided she'd had enough. She ran back to the house and hid under the porch. We called her a few times, but my heart just wasn't in it. It was almost time for my mother to pick me up on her way home from work. I sat on the porch and waited, wondering what she was going to say when she saw my scratched face and torn shirt. I didn't care if I never climbed another tree in my whole life.

Mom was pretty upset when she saw me, but there was one good thing that happened that day. Muff was still hiding when I climbed into the car and waved good-bye.

SPOTS

Once a year every grade in the Pleasant Street School spends a day at the zoo. Tim has gone six times because he is in the sixth grade. Caroline has gone four times. She missed one time when she skipped a grade. I should have gone twice already, but in first grade I sprained my ankle and had to stay home. Last year was my second chance to go, and I missed it again. While the rest of the kids were riding the bus to the city, I was home with a fever. While they were looking at elephants and lions, I was watching dumb game shows on television and coughing.

This year nothing was going to stop me. I drank gallons of orange juice and always wore my boots on rainy days, even though they look dumb. I even stayed away from Jamie Jamison. He is my best friend, but he never covers his nose when he sneezes. Jamie says he has hay fever, but I wasn't taking any chances.

"I don't know why you are so crazy about the zoo," Tim said. "I wish they would take us to a football game."

"I like animals," I said. "Mrs. Robbin says they have a new baby gorilla."

"What is all this about zoos?" asked Mrs. Albright. She was peeling potatoes for dinner because Mom was late.

"We're going to the zoo tomorrow," I told her. "Can you make me something special for my lunch?"

"I'll pack you a good lunch," Mrs. Albright said. "Don't I always?"

"But this is different. I missed last year, so this year I should have something really terrific."

"He wants to watch the monkeys so he'll know how to act," said Caroline, coming into the kitchen.

I made a face at her.

"See?" Caroline smirked. "He's already practicing."

Caroline and Tim laughed, but I was too excited

about the trip to be mad. Mrs. Albright wiped her hands and opened the refrigerator. "There's some chicken left from last night. That's good for a picnic lunch. And some grapes."

"I want a peanut butter sandwich, chicken, grapes, and a drink. And maybe some cake?" I suggested.

"I might just have some chocolate cake left," Mrs. Albright said. "Now run along and let me get dinner. Your mother will be tired when she gets home. She's been talking to the garbage collectors all day."

"Again?" I asked. I never want to be mayor when I grow up. Mom spends half her time talking to the water and sewer department, and the rest talking to the garbage collectors. They want to go on strike. That means they won't pick up the trash unless they get more money. Being a mayor is a lot of worries.

I took a bath and went to bed early that night so I wouldn't be tired the next day. But I couldn't sleep. My stomach itched.

I got up and looked at my stomach. There were funny-looking spots all over it. Maybe I was allergic to orange juice.

The next morning I got dressed before I came

out of my room. I knew if Mom or Dad saw those spots I would miss the zoo again. But lucky for me, Mom had already left. To talk to the garbage collectors again, I guess. Dad was reading the paper, Tim had early baseball practice, and Caroline had gotten a ride to school with Mom.

I gobbled up my breakfast even though I wasn't hungry. My luck was holding. Mrs. Albright was in the basement starting a wash, and Dad hardly looked up when I said good-bye.

"Have a good day at the zoo," Dad said.

Robbie banged on his high chair. "Robbie go zoo." Dad took Robbie's spoon away. "When you are big like Martin," he said. I used that minute to slip out the door. So far, so good.

As soon as the morning bell rang, Mrs. Robbin herded us all onto the bus. I gave a sigh of relief as the bus pulled away from the school. I was so happy that I didn't even care that I was sitting next to Marcia Stevens, the snobbiest girl in class.

Jamie was sitting behind us. As soon as the bus pulled away he sang in a loud voice:

First comes love,
Then comes marriage.
Then comes Martin with a baby carriage.

Some friend he was. I guess he was mad because I wouldn't sit with him when he was sneezing. Then I noticed Marcia was staring at me. "Ohh," she screamed. "What are those awful spots on your face?"

"Shh," I whispered. But she screamed even louder. "Mrs. Robbin. Martin has spots all over his face and I don't want to sit next to him."

Mrs. Robbin had been at the front of the bus trying to get everyone to sing "Row, Row, Row Your Boat." But when Marcia screamed, the bus became very quiet. Everyone was twisting around trying to look at me. I wished I could crawl under the seat and disappear.

Mrs. Robbin made her way back to my seat. She gave a deep sigh and put her hand on her head like she had a headache. "Martin, didn't you know you were sick before you got on the bus?" she asked.

"I thought maybe I was allergic to orange juice," I said. I wanted to explain about missing the zoo last year, and how it wasn't fair because I liked animals better than anyone in the class, but I didn't get the chance. "I'm very disappointed in you, Martin. I'm sure Caroline or Tim would never have done anything so thoughtless."

She shook her head and went to talk to the

driver. "Children, we are going back to school to drop off Martin before we continue our trip. He has the chicken pox."

Marcia scooted closer to the window. "If I get the chicken pox, I'll never speak to you again, Martin Snotgrass."

I crossed my fingers and made a wish.

❦ 7 ❦

CHICKEN POX AND SPELLING BEES

Except for missing the zoo, having the chicken pox wasn't all that bad. Dad wasn't too happy at first, though.

"How could you embarrass me that way?" he said. "I'm a doctor. I'm not supposed to let my child expose the whole town to chicken pox."

"Look at it this way, Dad," Tim joked, "Martin might have found you a whole lot of new patients."

Dad glowered for a minute, but then he laughed. "Next time you are sick, tell somebody. I'll take you to the zoo myself, if it's that important."

"I won't do it again," I promised meekly.

Mrs. Albright brought me my meals on a tray, and Mom moved an extra television into my room so I could watch all my favorite programs. But after a few days, it got pretty boring.

Caroline was in her room practicing for the county spelling bee. She was already the school champion. "I'll help you practice if you come in here," I called to her. I was pretty desperate for company.

"How can *you* help? You can't even read half the words," Caroline sneered. "Anyway," she said, sticking her head in the door, "I don't want to catch your germs."

"Dad says you've already been exposed. So it doesn't matter now."

"If I miss the spelling bee because I've got the chicken pox, I'll never forgive you," Caroline said.

"I didn't get sick on purpose, you know. I'm the one who missed the zoo. Three years in a row."

"I guess that was rotten luck," she admitted. "But you really didn't miss that much. All those animals. Whew," she said, holding her nose.

"I like animals," I said. "Maybe I'll work in a zoo when I grow up. Or maybe I'll be a forest ranger."

"I'm going to be rich and famous when I grow up," Caroline said.

"How are you going to do that?" I asked.

"I don't know yet. But I will be. You can come and visit me," she said grandly. "But you will have to leave all your animals at home. I don't want hair on my beautiful furniture."

She started to leave, but stopped at the door. "Guess what? Somebody is moving in next door."

"Really?" I climbed out of bed to look out my window. Sure enough, there was a moving van, and some men were carrying furniture into the house.

"Any kids?" I asked Caroline. The house had been empty for a long time. We didn't have many neighbors because we lived outside of town. Behind our house was a cornfield. Caroline's friend Mandy lived nearby, and Tim was old enough to ride his bike wherever he wanted to go, but there wasn't anyone around for me to play with. Jamie lived way over on the other side of town.

"I don't know." Caroline shrugged. "I haven't seen the people yet. Anyone would be better than the Flemmings, though."

We had all been happy when the Flemmings moved away. Mr. Flemming had a bald head and little squinty eyes. He came over a lot to borrow things. When he did, his eyes would dart around the room looking at everything. If Mom or Dad had anything new he would say he had something better at his house. So why was he always borrowing stuff?

Mrs. Flemming squealed a lot. "Ohh, that Robbie is the cutest baby," she would squeal. Then she would tickle him under the chin. As soon as Robbie got some teeth, he bit her finger.

Caroline and I sat by the window for a while, looking for clues about our new neighbors. It didn't look promising. The movers didn't unload a single toy or bike. After a while an old man came out of the house.

"Do you suppose he's the new neighbor?"

"He's too old to have any kids," Caroline said.

"Maybe he has grandkids that visit," I suggested.

"He looks grouchy," Caroline said.

"How can you tell from way up here?" I asked. My room was on the second floor of our house.

"Don't you know anything?" Caroline sighed. "Old people are always grouchy. They keep your balls if they get thrown into their yard, and yell at you if you walk on their grass. You'll know things like that when you are older, like me."

I figured Caroline ought to be an expert on grouches, since she is such a big one herself. But in this case it looked as though she was right. The old man suddenly walked over to the edge of his yard. He picked up a ball that Tim had forgotten, carried it into his house, and shut the door.

THE GROUCH IN THE GARDEN

Caroline did win the spelling contest. I had to stay home because I still had spots all over my face. Mom thought I would feel bad, so she told Mrs. Albright to let me stay up and watch a vampire movie on television. Tim was really mad. He had to go and watch Caroline with the rest of the family.

The movie was really terrific. The vampire kept changing into a bat, and when he was a man he had creepy eyes and lots of blood dripping from his teeth. It was so scary! Since I had to go to bed before the rest of the family got home, I left the light on in my room—but I put a book on top of my covers so it would look like I fell asleep reading.

The next day Caroline had her picture in the paper. The article said she was a pretty redhead who was very mature for her age. Her girlfriends came over and they read the article about a hundred times. I could have told them a few things. Now every time she passes a mirror she stops to fluff up her hair.

I was feeling better, so I decided I would go outside and talk to the new neighbor. He had used a Rototiller and dug up a spot for a garden. Now he was hard at work raking it smooth.

"Hi," I said, leaning on the fence. "I'm Martin Snodgrass. You haven't met me before because I've had the chicken pox. I'm better now, so I could help you if you want."

He shook his head and went right on working without looking up. "No, thanks," he grunted.

"What's your name?" I asked. I still hoped he would be friendly.

The man's back was slightly stooped, and his hair was thick and white. He had bushy eyebrows that made him look fierce. For several minutes he worked without answering, and I almost gave up and went back in the house. Then he straightened up and leaned on his hoe.

"My name is Harold DeWitt. I live alone, and I like it that way. I don't want any help. And I certainly don't want a bunch of kids running through my garden and trampling my flowers. I hope your parents have taught you to respect other people's property."

"Of course they have," I said. "But I wouldn't do that anyway. I like gardens. And I always walk carefully. I don't like to walk on any worms or ants."

Mr. DeWitt stared at me. For a second I thought I saw a tiny smile. Then he looked away. "I don't want to talk. I'm too busy."

"I could talk to you while you work," I suggested.

"Why don't you talk to someone your own age?" Mr. DeWitt said.

"There isn't anyone my age around here. Tim is at baseball practice, and Caroline has a bunch of girls in her room. Did you see her picture in the paper?"

Mr. DeWitt grunted something that might have been a yes. "Did you ever have your picture in the paper?" I asked.

He looked up from his work again. "No. Wouldn't have wanted to, either. What I do is my own business."

"If you get your picture in the paper everyone likes you because you are famous," I said.

"Don't think I'd want a friend who only liked me because I was famous. Anyhow, it's only important to be liked by one person." Mr. DeWitt went back to his work. "And that is yourself. Anyone else is nice, but not necessary. Now leave me alone. I have a lot of work to do."

"I told you he'd be grouchy," Caroline said later.

"Maybe he's just lonesome," I said.

"That's dumb." Caroline snorted. "If he was lonesome, he would be trying to make friends."

"Maybe he thinks all kids are awful," I said. "Like you think all old people are grouchy."

I thought about Mr. DeWitt a lot. Caroline might be an expert on being grouchy, but I knew something about being lonely. Being lonely could make you grouchy.

❧ 9 ❧

VINEGAR PANCAKES

In April Mrs. Robbin moved me up to the Lions reading group. That was the one Jamie was in, and he's one of the best readers in the class.

When Mrs. Robbin found out how unhappy I was about missing the zoo trip she gave me some books about zoo animals. I read them all. I learned that a giraffe has a black tongue, and lions in the wild only eat about once a week. When I told Mrs. Robbin how much I'd learned she gave me a reading test, and that's when she put me in the Lions. Before that I was a Raccoon.

"I'm proud of you," Mrs. Robbin said. And she didn't even mention Caroline.

April was also the month we tried to make Mom and Dad breakfast in bed. It was all Caroline's idea. She woke me up at five o'clock in the morning.

"Come to the kitchen," she whispered, "and be very quiet."

I sat up in bed. "What's the matter?"

"It's Mom and Dad's anniversary," she said importantly. "That means the day they got married. I heard them talking about it last night and I decided that we should make them breakfast in bed."

"Are you sure you know how?" I asked.

"Of course. I'm a girl. All girls know how to cook. I watch Mom all the time."

We woke up Tim and then together we trooped down to the kitchen.

"What should we make?" Tim asked, rubbing his eyes.

"Pancakes," Caroline said firmly. "Tim, you get the flour."

"How much?" he asked.

Caroline thought for a minute. "About five cups should be right. That would be a cup for each of us. I won't count Robbie. He doesn't eat much."

Tim opened the flour canister. "What cup should I use?"

"The measuring cup, dummy. Don't you know anything about cooking?" She rolled her eyes.

"Honestly, boys are so dumb."

"I knew it all the time." Tim sniffed. "I was just checking to see if you knew."

"Of course I knew. That's why I skipped the first grade, because I'm smart. They didn't let *you* skip."

"Just because you skipped doesn't make you the world's expert on everything," I said.

"I'm smarter than you any day," Caroline said. "I'll bet I can spell any word you can think of. Go on. Ask me."

"Mississippi," I said. "M-i-s-s-i-s-s-i-p-p-i," Caroline chanted. "That's not even hard, dog breath."

"Don't call me that," I shouted.

"Touchy, touchy." Caroline smirked.

"You are going to wake up Mom and Dad before we are ready," Tim warned.

"What should I do?" I asked crossly.

"You fix the tray," Caroline told me, "and make it look pretty."

I found the tray Mom used when we were sick, and covered it with one of our company napkins. Then I laid out the silverware and plates. Flowers would make the tray pretty. But the daffodils were finished blooming, and nothing else had started.

Mom had a row of African violets in her kitchen window. I knew she liked them because I heard her tell Dad how nice it was that they had all bloomed at the same time. I pushed a chair over to the window and picked them. They were too small for a vase, so I floated them in a bowl.

"I can't get this egg to crack," Caroline complained.

"You have to hit it hard," Tim said. "Like this."

"Oh, no," Caroline groaned. "You got pieces of shell in there."

We bent over the bowl and picked out pieces of eggshell. We were so busy that none of us noticed Robbie was up—until we heard the crash. A whole box of eggs was upside down on the floor. Gooey orange yolk was running under the refrigerator.

"Robbie!" we all yelled at the same time.

Robbie did what he always did when somebody yelled at him. He began crying at the top of his lungs.

"He's going to wake up Mom," Caroline wailed. "And we're not ready. Quick. Somebody get me the vinegar."

"You don't put vinegar in pancakes," Tim said.

"I watched Mom make a cake last week. She put some vinegar in the milk. She said it made it rich."

"Well, I can't find any," Tim said, peering into the cupboards.

"Pickle juice is vinegar," I suggested. "Maybe we could use that."

"Good idea," said Caroline. She gave Robbie a pickle to keep him happy and poured some pickle juice into the batter. She handed me the jar to put away, but I slipped on a broken egg. The jar fell on the floor with a crash loud enough to wake up a graveyard.

We heard the floor creak upstairs. Mom and Dad were up. I peeked in the bowl. "That looks awful. It smells awful, too."

"It's supposed to look like that. It tastes better when it's cooked," Caroline said.

Tim looked in the bowl. "I'm not eating sour pancakes," he said.

"I'm not either," I said.

"They are for Mom and Dad anyway." Caroline sniffed.

Mom and Dad walked in just then. Mom's face got sort of pale, and she backed out of the room. "I didn't see this," she said. "Tell me I'm still asleep."

Dad's face didn't look pale. It looked purple, like he was holding his breath. He looked at Mom. "Happy anniversary, dear," was all he said.

10

LOOSE TOOTH

Mom called us all into the kitchen three days before Mother's Day. "I want you to listen carefully. I do not want my breakfast in bed on Mother's Day. Understand? DO NOT FIX ME BREAKFAST!"

"Never?" I asked.

"Maybe when you are twenty-five." Mom sighed. "But not until then."

"How about lunch?" Tim asked.

Mom gave him a look. "It was just a joke, Mom," Tim said weakly.

Since we were not allowed to make breakfast, we had to think of another present. But we had a problem.

"I've only got seventy-five cents," Tim said.

"I've got a dollar. Maybe we could put all our money together," Caroline suggested. "How much do you have, Martin?"

"None," I admitted.

"Not a penny?" asked Tim.

"I had thirty-five cents yesterday. But I bought a candy bar. Gee, I forgot about Mother's Day."

"If you don't chip in some money, the present can't be from you," Caroline said.

"I could pay you back next week when I get my allowance," I pleaded.

Tim was looking at me. "I know how you can get some money."

"How?"

"You have a loose tooth, don't you? I could pull it out for you. Then when you put it under your pillow, you'll get fifty cents."

I wiggled the tooth with my tongue. If I pushed hard, it hurt.

"I don't think it's ready," I said.

"Let me see." Caroline wiggled the tooth.

"Ouch," I yelled. "That hurt."

"Don't be such a baby. It's either that, or the present isn't from you."

"I'll have to think about it," I said.

"If Martin gets his fifty cents we will have two dollars and twenty-five cents. What can we get for Mom?" asked Tim.

"Flowers," Caroline said in her bossiest voice. "I think a dozen roses would be nice. I saw them advertised. The ad said roses were the perfect gift."

It was settled. On Saturday we would go to the florist and buy the roses. That meant I had two days to get my tooth out. I looked in the bathroom mirror and wiggled my tooth hard. I could see there was some blood around it.

"I lost one of mine eating an apple," Tim said, following me into the bathroom. "All it took was one big bite."

"Did it hurt?" I asked.

"Of course not," Tim scoffed.

I went to the kitchen and got an apple from Mrs. Albright. I took a deep breath and bit down hard.

"Ouch," I moaned.

"Did it work?" asked Caroline.

I ran my tongue gently over the spot. The tooth was still there.

"How about gum?" suggested Caroline.

"I tried that once," Tim said. "It won't work. You'll have to let me tie a string around your tooth and pull it out."

I backed away with my hand over my mouth.

"It will only hurt for a second," Tim said. "Dad pulled one of mine that way. It was nothing."

"Remember," Caroline added, "if you don't get the money, the present isn't from you."

Tim got a piece of thread out of Mom's sewing basket. It took him three tries, but he finally got it tied. I hoped Mom would like her flowers. She'd better.

"Ready?" Tim asked.

I nodded and Tim pulled. But at the last minute I changed my mind and caught the string with my hand.

"Why did you do that?" Tim asked. "It would have been all over by now."

"I wasn't ready."

Tim snorted. Caroline smiled a little too sweetly. "Want me to hold your hands?"

I had to let Tim pull it. If I didn't, Caroline would tell the whole school I was a chicken.

"I'm ready now," I said as bravely as I could.

"You better be. I've got to go to baseball practice in a minute." He tied the string once more. I made myself stand perfectly still, arms at my side.

"Ye-ow!" I screamed, tasting blood.

"Where is the tooth?" Caroline asked. It wasn't

on the end of the string or on the floor.

I felt in my mouth. "It's still there."

"That's funny," Tim said. "Mine came right out when Dad did it."

"You had better go wash your hands, Tim," Caroline said. "Dad said a human mouth has more germs than a dog's."

Tim went to wash his hands. I went to the kitchen and sat at the table with my hands on my chin. If only I hadn't bought that candy bar.

Mrs. Albright was just putting on her coat to go home. "Why, Martin," she said, "what makes you so gloomy?"

I showed her the tooth and told her how we had tried to get it out.

"Land sakes, child," she said, reaching into her purse. "Why didn't you just ask me in the first place?" She handed me fifty cents.

"Thanks, Mrs. Albright. I'll pay you back as soon as my tooth comes out." I ran to tell Tim and Caroline that I had the money.

Three days after Mother's Day, my tooth fell out while I was eating macaroni and cheese.

11

CARNATIONS AND ROSES

The Saturday before Mother's Day we walked to the florist.

"Maybe we will have enough money to buy a pretty card," I said.

"Maybe," Caroline agreed.

The woman behind the counter beamed at us when we walked in. "I'll bet you want something for Mother's Day," she said. Then she brightened even more. "I recognize you. You are the mayor's children. You play ball," she said to Tim. Her eyes swung around to Caroline. "And you are the spelling champion." Finally she looked at me and her bright look faded. "What do you do? Play ball like your brother?"

"Tell her what we want," I whispered to Caroline.

"We want a dozen roses," Caroline said.

The woman looked startled. "Have you ordered them?"

"No," Caroline admitted. "We didn't know you had to."

"We sell so many roses on Mother's Day that we really do need an advance order. But I think we can manage something for the mayor. They are forty dollars a dozen."

"Forty dollars!" I guess the woman thought we were rich since our mother was the mayor. "Why do they cost so much?" I blurted out. "We can grow them right in our backyard."

The woman sniffed. "Our roses are special long-stemmed roses. We only sell them when they are just ready to open."

"What if they weren't so perfect," Caroline said. "What would you charge us then?"

"We don't sell them at all if they are not perfect. We have to think of our reputation. Why don't you tell me how much money you do have. Perhaps I can make you a nice bouquet."

"What do you have for two dollars and twenty-five cents?" Tim asked.

The woman coughed behind her hand the way

some grown-ups do when they don't want you to know you've said something dumb. "Our smallest bouquet is fifteen dollars," she explained. "But for two dollars I could fix you up a few carnations in a box. After all, it's the thought that counts, they say."

A few minutes later she handed us a long box. Inside were four carnations with pink edges, tied with a bow. I sniffed in the box.

"They smell nice," I said.

The woman took our money and smiled. "I'm sure your mother will like them."

I thought the carnations were nice, but Caroline and Tim were glum. We walked around the back of the building to take a shortcut home. There was a giant trash can in the alley.

"Hey, look at this," I yelled.

The can was nearly filled with roses. We couldn't believe our eyes. Just then a teenage boy came out of a house across the alley. "Have they dumped the flowers yet?" he called.

"Why are they in the garbage?" Tim asked.

"Those are the ones that aren't perfect," the boy said. "They are too old to sell. I get them for my Mom all the time. The owner doesn't care."

"We wasted all that money," Caroline complained as we picked out two dozen roses.

"Yeah," I said. "We could have bought Mom a box of candy."

"You'd have eaten it before we got home." Caroline laughed. "Then your teeth would fall out."

Everyone says your teeth will fall out if you eat too much candy. But what if they are falling out anyway? Does that mean you can eat a lot of candy, at least until the new ones come in? It was something to think about.

Of course we had to explain about all the flowers when we got home. We gave them to Mom a day early so she could put them in water.

"They are beautiful," she said. "But I think I like the carnations better."

"You like the carnations better than all these roses?" Caroline asked.

"I like them better because you bought them with your own money. Mrs. Albright told me Martin was even trying to pull out a tooth to help pay for them." She gave us all a mushy hug. "These carnations are as sweet as my children."

The roses died in a few days, but the carnations lasted a lot longer. Mom pressed them in a book and then put them in a box that held her favorite things.

"I wonder if all moms are as weird as ours," Caroline remarked. "I guess the people who make the advertisements don't really know very much about moms."

12

BLISTERS AND APHIDS

Mr. DeWitt's garden was starting to grow. From my bedroom window I looked down on neat rows of vegetables just poking through the ground. All around the borders Mr. DeWitt had planted flowers.

"I wish we could have a garden," I said one morning at breakfast.

Mom shook her head. "Your Dad and I don't have time for a garden."

"You wouldn't have to do any work," I said. "I would take care of it."

"You don't know anything about growing a garden." Caroline snorted.

"I'm not asking you." I glared at her. "Anyway, I can learn. Dad could show me what to do. Or maybe Mr. DeWitt. I'll bet he knows everything about gardens."

"Dad is too busy taking care of his sickies," Tim said. "And Mr. DeWitt is not going to teach you anything. Unless it's how to be a grouch."

"He might."

Mom sighed. "Tim, stop calling your father's patients sickies and Martin, I don't think you realize how much work a garden can be. It might be fun for a while, but you'd soon get tired of it."

"No, I wouldn't," I said. "It would give me something to do all summer. I'd be getting a lot of fresh air and exercise," I added, with a look at Dad. Fresh air and exercise were his favorite subjects. "Wouldn't it be better than sitting around all summer watching television?"

"It would be nice to have a few fresh vegetables this summer," Mom admitted. "But I still don't know...."

"There is a little space behind the garage." Dad spoke from behind his paper. "You can try a small one. Now, please, may I read my paper in peace?"

As if to answer, Robbie threw a spoonful of oatmeal. It landed *splat*, right on top of Dad's head.

Robbie clapped his hands.

The phone rang while Dad was mopping off his head. It was the hospital.

"Lucky for you, young man," Dad said, shaking his finger at Robbie. "I have to check one of my patients."

Robbie puckered. "Kiss Robbie," he said. It is hard to be mad at someone who has his lips stuck out for a kiss. Dad kissed him and left.

I went out to dig up some ground for the garden. This is going to be fun, I told myself. A half hour later I wasn't so sure. An hour later my shoulders ached, and there were big blisters on my hands.

"Don't pick at those," Mr. DeWitt said, walking over to my garden plot. "It will just make them worse."

I flopped on the ground. "I wanted a big garden like yours. But I can't even get the ground dug up."

"Isn't there someone to help you?"

"Mom had a meeting, and Dad had to go to the hospital. Tim and Caroline think I'm dumb to want a garden."

Without a word Mr. DeWitt turned and walked back to his garage. I was too exhausted to move. Caroline is right, I thought, I can't do anything. Not even grow a garden.

The sound of a motor brought me up with a jerk. Mr. DeWitt had come back with his Rototiller. Without a word he set to work and soon there was a dug-up square of land ready to be a garden.

"Thanks, Mr. DeWitt," I said. "That really helps."

He looked at me and shrugged. "By the way, see this little fellow?" He pointed to a ladybug sitting on a leaf of a bush. "Never kill one of them. They eat bugs that can harm your garden, like aphids." And then, without a word, he turned away and pushed his Rototiller back to his garage.

When Dad got back from the hospital he drove me to the garden center. I picked out seeds for lettuce, green beans, radishes, and onions. Then I bought some tomato and green pepper plants. I read the directions very carefully and planted everything in nice straight rows. Around the edges I planted marigolds. The man at the store said they were pretty and easy to grow.

I was just finishing when Mom came home. "Why, Martin, that's a beautiful job," she said. "It will be nice to have a salad right from the garden."

"If anything ever grows." Caroline sniffed. She had come out to see the garden with Mom. "Look, you have yucky bugs already."

"That's a ladybug," I told her. "They are good to have in a garden because they eat aphids."

Caroline looked at Mom. "Is that true?"

When Mom nodded, I said, "Of course it's true. Everyone knows that. Boy, are you ever dumb."

❧ 13 ❧

TEACHER SNODGRASS

Mrs. Robbin gave us
our last math test of the year. Everyone groaned,
but I was only pretending. Math is my favorite subject. I didn't want anyone to know it, though, in
case they thought I was weird. Jamie was the only
one who admitted he liked math. But Jamie is the
best in every subject. He even looks smart, so there
is no use pretending.

I saw Willie Smith's paper as we passed them up
to Mrs. Robbin. It was only half finished.

Just as Mrs. Robbin was telling us to take out our
science books, a message came from the office. Mrs.
Robbin looked quickly around the room. I slid

down in my seat so she wouldn't notice me.

"Martin, you'll be in charge while I am gone. Just lead the class in reading the chapter that starts on page one twenty-eight."

Before I could say a word, she was gone. I stood up and went to the front of the room. "Okay," I said, trying to smile. "Open your books to page one twenty-eight."

"Make us, Snotgrass." It was Willie, of course.

"Walter," I said, ignoring Willie, "will you read the first page?"

"Sure," Walter said. He stood up, grinning, and pretended to read:

> Doctor, doctor, come real quick,
> I touched Martin and I got real sick.

The whole class broke into laughter. My face grew redder and redder. Everyone was yelling. A paper airplane sailed over my head. If Mrs. Robbin came back now, I would be in big trouble.

I stepped to the door and looked out. "Quick, here comes Mrs. Robbin," I called.

In one second flat everyone was back in their seats, and Walter was reading from page 128: the right words this time.

After a minute Willie got up and looked out into the hall.

"You tricked us, Snotgrass. Mrs. Robbin isn't coming." He pushed me and my foot bumped the wastepaper basket next to Mrs. Robbin's desk. I reached down and picked it up. Then I turned it upside down right over Willie's head. Little balls of paper fell out and rolled on the floor.

I don't know who was more surprised, Willie or me. We both just stood there, Willie with the basket over his head, and me with my mouth hanging open. The class was roaring with laughter. We were still there when Mrs. Robbin came back.

We were both sent to the principal's office immediately.

"Martin," Mr. Higgenbottom said, "I'm disappointed in you." He tapped his pencil on the desk. "We've never had a problem with your brother or sister in this school. Wouldn't your parents be ashamed of you?"

I hung my head. But then Willie spoke up. "It was really my fault," he said. "I was calling him names and making fun of him."

Willie? Helping me?

Mr. Higgenbottom cleared his throat. "Ahem. Yes. Well, I'll let both of you boys off this time because it's so close to the end of the year. But this is the last time. Next time I will have to call your parents."

"I thought Mr. Higgenbottom was going to do something awful," Willie said on the way back to our room.

"How come you stood up for me?" I asked.

Willie grinned. "I have to keep up my reputation as a troublemaker, don't I? Besides, I like you."

"You like me?"

"Sure. Everyone does. You just have a funny name. Smith is a boring name. Nobody ever forgets a name like Snodgrass."

For the last week of school I was almost famous. There was even a song going around about me. It didn't make me mad like it would have before. Sometimes I would look up and see Willie grinning at me, and I would have to grin back.

> Teacher Snodgrass went to school.
> He got into trouble when he broke the rule.
> Teacher got mad.
> The principal got sick.
> Send for the doctor—quick, quick, quick.

❧ 14 ❧

ROBBIE'S FISH

I see about three days that we can take for a vacation," Dad said one morning at breakfast. He was looking at his calendar. "We will have to fit it in between Mrs. Olson's baby, Tim's baseball games, and Mom's meetings with the garbage collectors."

"How about New York City?" Mom said. "Art museums, Empire State Building, Statue of Liberty. It would be a learning experience for the kids."

"How about a camping trip?" Dad suggested. "We could all use a little fresh air and exercise."

Caroline and Tim groaned. "Don't we get a vote?" Caroline asked.

Dad sighed. "Where do you want to go?"

"How about Washington, D.C.?" Caroline asked.

"Caroline just wants to see where she'll be living when she's president," Tim joked. "How about the Baseball Hall of Fame in Cooperstown, New York?"

"You're all forgetting we only have three days," Dad said. "It has to be somewhere nearby."

"I'd like to go camping," I said.

Robbie banged his high chair with his spoon. "Robbie go tamping."

Mom looked glum. "For thousands of years people have struggled to gain a few comforts. Where do they go the first chance they get? Back to the woods! Cooking meals over smoky fires, getting sand in their shoes, and being eaten alive by bugs."

I caught Dad's eye and grinned. We had all heard this speech before. Last year. And the year before. And probably the year before that.

Dad hung the calendar back on the wall. "I think we had better go camping."

"Never," Mom said.

Three weeks later we were setting up our tents at Lake Tippiconda. "We could be in a plush hotel room getting room service," Mom grumbled, as

Dad drove the last tent stake into the ground.

"You know you always enjoy it after we get everything set up."

Mom looked doubtful. "Why don't you go fishing while I brew some coffee?"

Dad's face brightened. He loves to fish. "Good idea. Who wants to come along? Maybe we can catch some fish for dinner."

"We do," Caroline, Tim, and I shouted.

Robbie tugged at Dad's sleeve. "Robbie catch fish."

"Wouldn't you rather stay and help Mom?" Dad sighed.

"No!" Robbie stomped his foot. "Robbie catch fish."

"All right," Dad agreed. "But you have to be very quiet and not scare the fish."

I held Robbie's hand as we walked to the lake. We all had poles. Even Robbie had a bamboo pole with a string so he could pretend he was fishing.

When we got to the lake Caroline turned to me. "I'll bet my sticker book against your new soldier that I catch a bigger fish than you do."

"What are you going to do with my soldier?"

"I'll make him go out on dates with my fashion dolls. Or I'll pretend they are having a wedding."

"Soldiers don't go out with stupid fashion dolls." I snorted.

"You're just scared you won't win, dummy," Caroline said.

"I am not."

"Will you two please pipe down?" Dad said.

"It's a bet," I whispered. "And stop calling me dummy."

"Okay, dog breath," Caroline said.

I poked her arm. "Don't call me that either."

"Dad," Caroline wailed, "Martin hit me just because I said I could catch a bigger fish."

"I did not," I spluttered. "She keeps calling me names."

"Caroline, stop calling your brother names. And Martin, don't hit your sister. And both of you keep quiet," Dad said.

Robbie started to cry. "Worm hurt," he blubbered.

"You have to use a worm to catch a fish," Dad tried to tell him. "Not that there are any fish within miles of here by now."

Robbie kept right on bawling. "Worm hurt."

"I have an idea," I said. I ran back to camp, got a hot dog from Mom, and ran back. "Look, Robbie. Maybe the fish will like hot dogs."

Robbie smiled. Dad sat Robbie next to him and put his line in the water. Caroline was humming "Here Comes the Bride."

"Dad, make her stop singing that."

"Martin," Dad said, "I thought we came here to fish."

"We did."

"Then why are you making enough noise to scare away every fish for a hundred miles?"

For a while everyone was quiet. Then I heard Caroline singing softly so only I could hear:

Down by the river, down by the sea,
Martin got in trouble, and he blamed it on me.
I told Ma, Ma told Pa.
Martin got a licking, so ha, ha, ha.

Before I could make her stop, Robbie started shouting.

"He couldn't have caught anything," Dad exclaimed. Just then the biggest fish I ever saw jumped out of the water. Dad jerked the line and the fish flopped onto the bank next to Robbie.

Robbie started crying again. "Fishy hurt."

"How did it go?" Mom asked when we came

back from the fishing trip.

"Don't ask," Dad muttered.

We sat down to a dinner of cold chicken and potato salad Mom had packed at home.

"Robbie caught a fish, but he made us throw it back," I said.

"It was a whopper," Tim said.

"Did you really catch a fish?" Mom asked Robbie.

Robbie grinned happily.

"Robbie wet pants."

Dad looked at Mom. "Next year we are going to the fanciest hotel you can find. Alone," he added grimly.

SPIDERS AND SKUNKS

By the time we finished dinner and built a campfire to roast marshmallows, Dad was in a better mood. He put another marshmallow on his stick and held it over the glowing coals. "This is more like it," he said.

"It's kind of romantic." Mom leaned her head on his shoulder.

"I wouldn't go quite that far." Dad swatted a mosquito. He picked up Robbie, who had fallen asleep. "Maybe we all ought to get ready for bed. We can get up early and take a hike."

Mom looked at us. "Are you sure you won't be afraid by yourselves?"

"Of course not," Tim said. Caroline and I shook our heads. This year we had taken two tents. Robbie, Mom, and Dad were sleeping in one, Caroline, Tim, and I in the other.

"Okay," Dad said heartily. "We will only be a few steps away if you need us. See you in the morning."

"I'm leaving my flashlight on," Caroline said as we crawled into our sleeping bags.

"Well, don't shine it in my eyes," Tim grumbled. It was quiet for a minute as we all tried to find a spot without a rock poking in our backs. I was glad Caroline was leaving her flashlight on. She had it pointed at the top of the tent. Nothing ever bothered Tim. Next he'd want to tell ghost stories.

"I've got a good idea," Tim whispered. "Let's tell ghost stories." Suddenly he jumped up and screamed.

"W-what's the matter?" I said. Then I saw it and scrambled right out of my sleeping bag. Over our heads, hanging down from a strand of silk, was a big hairy spider. I like bugs. I like to watch them scurry around looking for food, and if I pick up a rock with bugs under it I put it back carefully so I don't disturb them. But even I do not like big hairy spiders hanging over my face in a dark, creepy tent. Just then the spider dropped to the ground and skittered away under the blankets. I started to shake them out.

Tim and Caroline were hollering for Dad as loudly as they could.

"Spider," Tim gasped as Dad burst through the tent flap.

"You mean to say all this fuss is about a little spider?" Dad said. "I thought you were being attacked by a bear."

"But, Dad." Tim was backing out of the tent. "It was huge. I think it was a tarantula or something."

"There are no tarantulas around here," Dad said.

"Well, whatever it was," Caroline announced, "I'm not sleeping in here until you find it."

Dad and I shook out blankets, shoes, and clothes. No spider.

"He must have crawled out," Dad said.

"I'm not sleeping in this tent," said Caroline. She folded her arms across her chest.

"But we've looked everywhere," Dad said.

"It's still in there"—Tim shuddered—"waiting until we go to sleep."

"Dad, are there any bears around here?" I asked. If Dad had come running because he thought we were being attacked by a bear, there must be some around.

"Of course not," Dad said. He looked at the

three of us shivering in our pajamas. "You all might as well sleep with us tonight. Tomorrow we'll search your tent in daylight."

"I didn't know you were afraid of spiders," I said to Tim as we were bringing our sleeping bags to the other tent.

"If you want to live," Tim hissed, "don't you dare say a word to anyone."

"I wouldn't do that," I said quickly. "I was just surprised. I thought you weren't afraid of anything."

"I'm afraid of lots of things."

"Like what?"

"Like not being able to throw the ball right and everyone laughing at me."

"That would never happen."

"It could. Anyway," Tim said, "I worry about it."

I snuggled down in my sleeping bag. Maybe, I thought, if you were famous, you always had to worry about staying famous. Still, it would be nice to be famous for a few minutes. Just to see what it was like.

Dad had to make three trips carrying stuff out of his tent to make room for all of us. "Now," he asked, "are there any more problems?" He reached over and turned off the camp light. "Good. Let's get some sleep."

For a second it was quiet. Then a small voice spoke up. "Robbie wet pants."

"Again?" Dad roared.

"I think you took the diapers to the other tent," Mom said.

Dad sat up and put his head in his hands. He didn't say a word. Finally he got up and stumbled out into the night. "Oh no! OHHH, NOOO," he yelled.

We all knew what had happened. There is no mistaking that smell. There had been a skunk out there, and Dad had startled it on the way to the other tent.

❧ 16 ❧

MILK BATHS AND PUMPKINS

The forest ranger Mom called suggested milk baths or tomato juice baths to get rid of the smell. Everyone but Dad piled into the car and drove to the only store nearby that was open at night. The clerk gave Mom a look as he rang up the five gallons of milk and four big cans of tomato juice. Mom acted like it was perfectly natural to be out in the middle of the night with four sleepy kids buying gallons of juice and milk.

As we climbed back in the car she burst into very un-Mom-like giggles. "I would love to know what he was thinking," she said, "wouldn't you?"

Dad spent the rest of the night washing in the

lake. He was a pretty good sport about it, although we could hear him mumbling things like "Never, never again."

We drove home the next morning. The smell wasn't too bad, but Mom made Dad drive with all the windows open. The skunk had missed the tent, but no one said it was nice that we could use it again. For the first few days that we were home Dad took a lot of baths. Even so, it was almost a week before you couldn't tell that he had been in a room.

I was glad to get back to my garden. I rushed out to check it as soon as we got home. Mr. DeWitt was out working in his garden as usual.

"Hi," I waved. Mr. DeWitt looked up and nodded, then went back to his work. A minute later he came over to the edge of his yard.

"I have too many pumpkin plants," he said gruffly. "Would you like a couple for your garden?"

"That would be great," I said. "I can grow my own jack-o'-lanterns."

He managed a smile. "You might want to stake up those tomato plants, too," he said, "or your tomatoes will sit on the ground and rot."

He went to his garage and returned with some tall stakes. He helped me drive them into the ground and tie the plants to them.

"You are doing a nice job with your garden," he said. "I figured you would be tired of it by now."

"I like to watch things growing," I said.

Mr. DeWitt looked at me for a while. "I guess I feel the same way."

"Is that why you have such a big garden for just you?" I asked.

"It keeps me busy," he snapped. "Got used to growing a big garden on the farm."

"You have a farm?"

"Used to. I sold it. Too much for one person to keep up."

"Don't you have any family?" I asked. I'd never seen anyone visit.

"I have a son. Used to have a son. He moved out to California. Wants to be an actor."

"Wow. A real actor," I said.

"It's ridiculous." Mr. DeWitt snorted. "Grown man playing around. Worked all my life to have the farm to leave him. But he doesn't want it."

"Maybe he didn't like being a farmer. I wouldn't like it if my Dad made me do something I didn't like when I grew up."

"That's different," Mr. DeWitt snapped. "Your father has four children. Paul was all I had."

"But now you don't have anybody," I pointed out. I guess that made him mad. He turned, and without another word, went into his house. I waited for a long time, but he didn't come back out.

❧ 17 ❧

WORMS AND FLUFFY FROSTING

Mom was happy because at last the meetings with the garbage collectors were over. We wouldn't have a town full of garbage after all. There was a big picture of Mom in the paper, shaking hands with the leader of the garbage collectors. In the same paper was a picture of Tim. He pitched the championship game against Springdale. The score was fifteen to one. The caption under the picture read: "Snodgrass Wipes 'Em Out." I wondered how Tim would have felt if it said: "Snotgrass Wipes 'Em Out."

Dad was busy with his patients. Three more ladies were about to have babies, and one of them was expecting twins. Dad said that at the rate the town was growing, Mom would have to hire some more garbage collectors.

I think all Dad's patients who are expecting babies should spend a week with Robbie to see what they're in for. When he was little all he did was spit up and drool down the front of his shirts. He doesn't do that anymore. Now he gets into things. Last week he took a whole box of stickers I'd been collecting and stuck them all over the dining room wall. When I yelled at him he just stuck out his lips for a kiss. I sometimes wonder what great things Robbie is going to do. Nothing is showing up yet, but I'm sure it will. After all, his name is Snodgrass. And that means famous, except for me.

After what Mr. DeWitt said about his son, I found myself wondering if Mom and Dad were unhappy that I couldn't do anything great. Maybe they were really disappointed in me and just too polite to say so. I had to do something terrific soon. If only there were some way to get my picture in the paper.

It had rained all night, but the next morning—Saturday—the sun was shining and there were a lot of worms stuck on the driveway. Each one I picked up I took to the garden because Mr. DeWitt said they help keep the soil broken up. I figured that since I was saving their lives they would probably work extra hard in my garden.

Caroline came out and watched for a few minutes. She made a face. "Worms are slimy," she said. "And they make your hands stink."

"They are good for the garden," I told her. "They make the dirt softer."

"I'll bet you just made that up," Caroline said.

"I did not. You don't know everything." I saw another worm and picked it up. "This makes twenty-two lives I've saved today," I said, dangling the worm in front of her face.

Caroline jumped back and screamed. "I'm going to tell Mom."

"Go ahead, tattletale."

"Okay, I will." Caroline ran back to the house yelling, "Mom, Martin is sticking worms in my face."

Mom came out of the house holding Robbie. "Caroline, don't tattle," she said. "And Martin, stop teasing your sister. Listen you two, your father is about to leave for the hospital and I have to run to the store to get some birthday candles. I'll only be gone a few minutes, and I want you both to watch Robbie."

"We will," I promised.

"It's my burpday," Robbie announced.

"I know," I said. "Mom is baking you a birthday cake."

Mom backed the car out of the garage. "I left the frosting bowl in the kitchen," she called. "You can lick the beaters."

We took Robbie into the house. Caroline took one beater and gave the other to Robbie. I scraped off what was left in the bowl. It was fluffy chocolate frosting, my favorite kind.

"You just licked your fingers and you didn't wash your hands," Caroline screamed. "You've got worm juice in your frosting."

"Delicious," I said, smacking my lips, but really I had suddenly lost my appetite for frosting.

A second later I forget about worms and frosting. Just as Caroline was saying, "Hey, where did Robbie go?" there was a loud crash from the living room.

🙚 18 🙘

WHERE'S ROBBIE?

Oh, no," Caroline groaned. "Mom's best fern. She's going to kill us."

The fern was tipped over and dirt had spilled all over the rug. Robbie was happily pulling the leaves off the plant and putting them on his head.

"Robbie make hat."

"Maybe we can scoop up all the dirt and replant it," I suggested. "We can vacuum and Mom won't ever know."

Caroline ran to get the vacuum cleaner. I put the plant back into the pot and patted dirt around it. It didn't look too bad when I was done, although there were a few broken stems. I set it back on the table while Caroline vacuumed up the dirt.

"That looks okay." Caroline snapped off the switch.

"I'll put it away," I said, taking the vacuum. Robbie had disappeared again.

"He's probably in my room," Caroline wailed. I stuck the vacuum in the hall closet and followed her to her room. Robbie was there all right, pulling all the clothes out of Caroline's drawers.

"Why did he have to pick my room?" Caroline grumbled. "No one would have even noticed in yours."

"I'll take him outside and play with him," I offered. "Come on, Robbie. What would you like to do?"

"Eat burpday cake," Robbie answered.

"That's for later," I said. "We'll have a big party, and then we'll eat cake. How about a ride in your wagon?"

Robbie loved to have someone pull him in his wagon. I pulled him all around the yard. He was only two, but he was heavy and it was hot. After a couple of times around I stopped under a tree to rest. Robbie pointed to the cornfield. "Ride in the corn," he said.

"We can't," I told him, wishing Mom would

hurry up and get back. "It's muddy and we'd get lost. I've got a better idea. Let's make a castle in your sandbox."

The sand was still wet from the rain, so it stuck together just right. Robbie took his bucket and filled it with sand.

Caroline came out of the house at last. "Let's make a fancy sand castle," she said, "with towers and moats like we do at the beach."

I went inside for plastic knives and some paper cups. Before long we had a pretty good castle started in the sandbox. Robbie kept crashing his dump truck into the back of it, trying to make a road, but the front was smooth and square.

Finally Mom came home.

"We make castle." Robbie beamed.

"Why, it's beautiful," Mom said.

"I can't get the bridge over the moat to look right," I said.

Mom's a pretty good castle builder herself. She knelt down beside us and started to shape the bridge. "I think if we stick this piece of cardboard in the side of the castle and cover it with sand, it will do the trick," she said.

We worked for a few minutes before Mom stood up and brushed the sand from her hands. "I ought to get the camera and take a picture of it before Robbie knocks it down." She looked around. "Where's Robbie?"

"He was right here a minute ago," I said. The yard was empty. Robbie was nowhere in sight, and there was only silence when we called.

19

HAPPY BURPDAY!

A chill ran down my back. The cornfield!

"I know where he is," I told Mom. "I was pulling him in the wagon and he wanted to go into the cornfield. I bet that's where he went."

Mom nodded. "Caroline," she said, "you ask the neighbors if they've seen Robbie. Martin and I will check the cornfield."

Mom and I ran to the edge of the field. Mom called again and again. The only sounds we heard were the caw of a startled crow and the buzz of insects. Only a few steps into the field the house was completely hidden from view. It was like being in a thick forest. Poor little guy, I thought. He must be scared to death.

"I think we need help," Mom said. "I'm going back to the house to make some calls. Don't go into the cornfield. Just walk along the edge of the field and keep calling. He might hear you."

While Mom was gone I looked down every row as far as I could see. I called and called. Poor Robbie. What a rotten way to spend a birthday, I thought.

An idea came into my head. I tried to ignore it, but this was the chance I'd been waiting for. If I could find him first, I would be a hero. I'd get my picture in the paper for sure. I could see it all now: "Martin Snodgrass, Hero!"

I took a step into the cornfield.

"Better not. Next they'll be looking for you."

"Mr. DeWitt. I didn't see you coming."

"Your sister told me what happened. I thought maybe I could help find the little fellow," he said gruffly.

Mom came back with two of the sheriff's deputies. "Better stay here," one of them said kindly. "We'll split up and search. Don't worry. We'll find him."

"Take all day," Mr. DeWitt growled. "That

field's over a hundred acres. What you need is a helicopter."

The deputy looked at the sea of cornstalks, all higher than my head. "You know," he said thoughtfully, "you may be right." He sent the other deputy back to the car.

Dad came home just as we heard the *putt-putt* of the helicopter flying over the field. Mom had called him at the hospital.

I watched the helicopter crisscross the field. Our neighbors were gathering and one of the deputies told everyone to spread out around the field in case Robbie came out.

Caroline came over to me. "I'll never get mad at him again when he gets into my things."

"Me neither," I promised. "I don't care who finds him. I don't even want my picture in the paper."

Caroline gave me a funny look. "What are you talking about? And why are you scratching your hands like that?"

I looked at my hands. Tiny white bumps were popping out all over them.

"Poison ivy," Mr. DeWitt said, coming over. "Get up to the house and wash your hands," he ordered. "Use plenty of soap and hot water. Wash them three or four times. Go on," he urged when I hesitated. "It will only help if you do it right away. They won't find him any quicker because you are standing here."

I ran back to the house and started scrubbing my hands at the kitchen sink. After three hard washings with dish detergent I figured I'd done all I could. Just then I caught sight of the birthday cake on the counter. It looked so sad sitting there with a great big hunk missing out of one side. A big piece missing? When did that happen? I was sure Robbie hadn't gotten into the cake before.

Then I noticed a chocolate smear on the door leading down the hall.

Robbie was sound asleep on the bathroom rug, his face covered with chocolate frosting. He must have come back inside to go to the bathroom. But he had stopped to sample some cake and hadn't made it in time. I gathered him up, wet pants and all, in a great big hug.

"Martin," he said sleepily, "Robbie wet pants."

I didn't wait to change him. I just ran outside with Robbie in my arms. There was a big cheer from the crowd when they saw him.

"Wow," he said happily. "Robbie have big burpday party."

20

A FARMER IN THE FAMILY

Robbie was right. It was a big party. Half the crowd stayed to watch him blow out his candles on what was left of the cake. We had the party outdoors so everyone could come, and some newspaper photographers took a lot of pictures of Robbie. I didn't really care that I wasn't in any of them.

Dad sprayed medicine on my hands. He said it was a good thing Mr. DeWitt had known just what to do. Dad asked Mr. DeWitt to stay for dinner, and he did. Tim came home from baseball practice just as we sat down to eat. He had missed the whole thing. Dad told the story again, making it sound like I'd done something really clever to find Robbie, instead of it just being luck. Nobody mentioned that I was the one who had started everyone looking in the cornfield in the first place.

After dinner Dad and Mr. DeWitt and I went outside to look at my garden.

"You've got a nice family," Mr. DeWitt told Dad. "And that Martin has really got a green thumb."

"We've been getting fresh vegetables all summer," Dad said. "It's nice to have a farmer in the family."

Mr. DeWitt's face looked sad, and I remembered what he'd said about wanting his son to be a farmer. But then he smiled.

"I've been watching those pumpkins you've got growing," he said to me. "You ought to think about entering them in the county fair."

I did have some really huge pumpkins, but I'd never thought about the fair. "Do you think they'd win?"

"They might. They are bigger than any of mine. I could show you how to make them really nice. You'll want to turn them gently now and then so they don't get a flat spot. And put several layers of newspaper under them. This will protect the pumpkins from bugs and rot."

I saw a flash of yellow at the edge of the field. It looked like a kitten. "Dad," I said, "I think there's a kitten in the cornfield."

I went to the edge of the field and tried to coax it out. "Here, kitty, kitty," I called. But it wouldn't come.

"Someone must have dumped it at the edge of town," Mr. DeWitt said.

"If I catch it, could we keep it?" I pleaded.

Dad shook his head. "You're not old enough. And Mom wouldn't want its hair all over everything."

"You could put an ad in the paper if you catch it," Mr. DeWitt said. "Maybe you could find it a good home. But you'd better get it soon. If you don't it will be too wild to be a good pet."

"I could try putting a bowl of food out at night. Maybe it will see we are friendly."

For the next few days Mr. DeWitt and I set out food and water. Every morning the dishes were empty, but the kitten stayed in the cornfield. All we ever saw was a flash of yellow.

Mr. Dewitt helped me put newspapers under the pumpkins and turn them so they would grow nice and round. One of the pumpkins was already so big I couldn't lift it by myself.

"I'm going to have some company," Mr. DeWitt

said one day. "My son is coming for a visit. I want you to meet him. After all, it was because of you that he is coming."

"Because of me?"

"Because of what you said that day. You see, my father raised me to take over the farm. And I did. But I took over the farm because I loved farming. It was what I wanted to do. I guess I just figured my son should be the same. But we are all different. I forgot that for a while and almost lost my only family. I didn't even know he had married. I'm going to be a grandfather."

After Mr. DeWitt went home I went to the garage to put away the hoe. I saw a flash of yellow under Dad's workbench.

"Here, kitty," I called. It didn't move. When I reached under the bench, it only mewed and trembled. Then I saw why. One leg was bent at a funny angle. The kitten was hurt.

21

DAFFY

I stood for a minute, holding the kitten in my arms. Dad was a doctor, but he was busy seeing his patients. Anyway, a people doctor might not know about kittens. Mr. DeWitt was sitting on his porch. I ran over to his house.

Mr. DeWitt took the kitten and gently felt her leg. "It's broken. But I think we can fix it."

I followed him into his house and watched him put a splint on the kitten's leg. His hands were gentle, and he talked softly to the kitten while he worked. The house looked a lot different from when the Flemmings had lived there. The last time I'd seen this kitchen there were frilly curtains on the windows and shelves to show off Mrs. Flemming's collection of glass animals. Now the house looked very plain and empty. Lonely. I was glad his son was coming for a visit.

Mr. DeWitt heated up some milk for the kitten. Even though the kitten couldn't stand, it lapped up the milk. Mr. DeWitt held the kitten in his arms and sat down in an old rocking chair.

"We will have to make her a box. You could keep it in your garage. But the kitten will need a lot of care until her leg heals. I'll help you."

The kitten curled up in his lap, her leg sticking out because of the splint, and began to purr. "She needs a name," said Mr. DeWitt.

"If I give her a name I might get too attached to her," I said. "And Mom and Dad said I couldn't keep her."

"We have to call her something. And I suspect you're going to get attached to her, name or not. How about something yellow for a name?"

"Lemon? Sunshine? Mustard? I've got it. How about Daffodil?"

"Daffodil," Mr. DeWitt said. "I like that. We could call her Daffy for short."

"How did you know how to take care of her?" I asked.

"You learn to take care of your animals on a

farm," Mr. DeWitt said. "For the big problems I called the vet. But most of the time I did things myself."

"I'd like to have a farm when I grow up," I said. "I'd have a cat and a dog and a horse and rabbits and cows. Maybe even a goat."

"What if your wife doesn't want all those animals around?" Mr. DeWitt teased.

"I'll just ask her first, 'Which would you rather have, a horse or a baby?' If she says a horse, I'll marry her."

It didn't take long for Daffy to start hobbling around, even though her leg was still bandaged. I liked to watch Mr. DeWitt with Daffy. Daffy liked him, too. After he changed her bandage, she would curl up in his lap and sleep.

At last it was time for the county fair. My best pumpkin was smooth and orange, without a single spot. It was so heavy Dad and Mr. DeWitt had to help me carry it. They put it on a table with a lot of other pumpkins and a lady gave it a number. There were a lot of other vegetables there, too, and a man and two ladies were doing the judging. They walked along looking at the displays and writing on little notepads. Now and then they would stop to talk to each other, and then ribbons would be placed on the winning fruits or vegetables.

At last they came to the pumpkins. One of the other pumpkins was bigger than mine.

"Don't worry," Mr. DeWitt said. "Yours is the best one on the table."

The judges kept looking at the bigger pumpkin and then at mine, as though they couldn't decide. Then one of the judges rolled the larger pumpkin around to check it, and I saw a flat spot on one side.

The judge pulled out a blue ribbon and stuck it on my pumpkin.

"You won." Dad grinned.

Mr. DeWitt patted my back. "You did a good job," he said.

Just then I saw the photographer from the newspaper. I tucked in my shirt and smoothed back my hair with my hands.

"The pumpkin is too heavy to move," the photographer said to the judges. "Let's just put the other winners around it." Prize-winning tomatoes, cabbages, peppers, and squash were placed around the pumpkin. I edged over to the table. Without even a glance in my direction, the photographer snapped the picture, put his camera away, and left.

The next day the picture was in the paper—on the very last page. You could hardly even see the pumpkin behind all the other vegetables, but Mom

clipped the picture anyway and put it in the family scrapbook.

"You worked hard for that ribbon," Mom said. "You should be very proud of it." She put her arm around my shoulders. "I have a surprise for you."

"You do?"

"Dad and I have been talking. We've been watching you these last few months. You have done a lot of growing up. You've been very responsible about your garden and taking care of Daffy. We know how much you love her, so we've decided to let you keep her."

That was what I'd been hoping to hear for weeks. But now it didn't seem right.

"What's the matter?" Mom said. "You've been asking for a pet for years."

"I think Mr. DeWitt needs Daffy more than I do. He hasn't got anyone else. But I have to pretend you said no, or he won't take her. Would that be all right?"

Mom gave me a kiss.

"Why did you do that?" I asked.

"Because, Martin Snodgrass, you are one of the nicest people I know."

A person doesn't have to have his picture in the paper to feel really good inside.

22

ROBBIE LIKES MARTIN

I was sound asleep one Saturday morning when I heard a funny noise. Slurp. Slurp. Then something wet dripped on my face. My eyes shot open.

Robbie popped another grape into his mouth.

I looked at my clock. "Robbie," I groaned, "why are you sitting on my bed eating grapes at six o'clock in the morning?"

"Robbie wake up," he explained.

"I can see that."

Robbie patted my face with sticky fingers and dived in for a kiss. I kissed him and wiped my mouth on the sheet. It seems like every time he kisses me his nose is running.

"I have an idea. Why don't you go wake up Caroline?" I said.

"Robbie likes Martin."

"I like you, too. But not at six o'clock in the morning." I sighed. "You're wet."

Robbie climbed up and sat down hard on my stomach with his wet pajamas. "Get up, Martin. Get up."

"Okay," I said. I dragged myself out of bed. I padded to the bathroom, holding Robbie by the hand. I peeled off his diaper. I wiped his nose. I got a pair of underpants for him. He wears a kind called training pants. They're thick in the middle in case of accidents. Robbie has a lot of accidents.

I made us each a bowl of cereal. Robbie gobbled his down, not counting what landed on the floor, and gave me a big grin between bites. No wonder no one ever noticed me. Caroline was smart, Tim was athletic, and Robbie was cute. I was just the one in the middle.

I wiped up the mess on the floor and turned on the television. Just my luck. It was so early even cartoons weren't on. I snapped off the television.

"You'll have to play for a while," I said.

"Martin play, too," Robbie said.

"Okay. What do you want to play? Want to build something with your blocks?"

"Play doggie." Robbie grinned. He got down on his knees and began to bark.

By the time everyone got up, I was ready for a nap.

"I have to go grocery shopping," Mom said. "Dad will be at the hospital, so you will all have to go with me. We can drop Tim off for swim team practice on the way."

Caroline and I both groaned. "Why do we have to go?" Caroline demanded.

"You like to eat, don't you?" Mom asked. "And if I left you two home together you would probably kill each other before I got back."

Robbie fell asleep immediately in his car seat. A few minutes later, Mom pulled the car into a space in front of McNaulty's grocery store.

Jamie Jamison and his mother were loading groceries into their car. Now I was glad my mother had made us go. It was the first time I had seen Jamie all summer. He had been away at camp.

"Mom, can I invite Jamie over tomorrow? Maybe he could stay all night. We could sleep outside in the tent."

"That sounds like a nice idea. I'll talk to his

mother. Maybe he can come for dinner."

Caroline groaned and slid down in the seat.

"What's the matter with you?" Mom asked.

"Another boy in the house. Don't you think there are enough boys already? I am surrounded by dumb boys," she said dramatically.

"That will be enough, Caroline," Mom said firmly. "Besides, the boys will be sleeping out in the tent, so they won't be bothering you."

Mom got out of the car to talk to Mrs. Jamison, and I made a face at Caroline. "I don't say anything when your creepy friends come over," I said.

"My friends are not creepy," Caroline sniffed.

"My friends are not dumb," I said. "Neither am I. And if you don't stop calling me dumb, I'm going to put worms in your bed."

"I'm going to tell Mom," Caroline said.

"Then I'll do it for sure," I said.

"You wouldn't dare."

"Stinky, slimy worms, slithering all over your sheets. They'll go between your toes and crawl in your hair."

Caroline shivered, but when Mom got in the car she didn't say a word.

"Jamie will be over tomorrow afternoon," Mom said, "at about four o'clock. His mother said he can spend the night."

Mr. DeWitt was out in his yard with Daffy when we got home. She was almost well, except for a little limp. Once in a while she came over to visit me. She never stayed very long, though. After my birthday I don't think she will come anymore. I heard Mom and Dad talking about getting me a puppy. I'm not supposed to know yet.

Mr. DeWitt smiled and waved when we drove up. Even Caroline and Tim talk to him now. As soon as we got home Caroline headed over to Mr. DeWitt's house, probably to tell him how awful I am. I just waved and headed into the house to get the tent. I knew Mr. DeWitt wouldn't believe her because when he introduced me to his son he said, "This is my best friend, Martin."

23

MARTIN IN THE MIDDLE

By four o'clock the next day the tent was set up in the backyard. Tim had helped me. "I did this a few times when I was your age," he said. He sounded like he wished he was my age again. I made a final check. There were two sleeping bags, a flashlight for each of us, comic books, games, and some potato chips and marshmallows for snacks.

The kitchen smelled like spaghetti sauce, Jamie's favorite dinner. I went into the living room to wait.

At five o'clock Mom came home from an emergency meeting about the city budget. I was still waiting. The phone rang just as she walked in.

"That was Mrs. Jamison," Mom said. "Jamie won't be able to come. She thinks he's coming down with the flu. He lives next door to Marcia Stevens and she was sick last week."

I might have known Marcia would find some way to get even. She had the chicken pox right after I did and had never forgiven me. "I'll sleep out by myself," I announced.

"All by yourself?" Mom looked doubtful. "Are you sure you won't be scared?"

"Of course not. I'm not a baby," I said.

"I know you're not," Mom said, "I just thought it would be more fun with somebody else. Maybe Caroline or Tim would like to sleep out with you."

I shook my head. "They are not company," I said. "Tim would tell ghost stories and Caroline would want me to play with her fashion dolls."

After dinner we watched a movie on television. It was about a werewolf who hung around in the woods waiting for someone to bite. We don't have any woods around our house, but the cornfield would be a good place to hide. I shivered.

"Still sleeping out by yourself?" Caroline asked after the movie.

"Of course I am. Why not?" I said. I whistled as I headed out the door.

It was dark outside. There were clouds covering up the moon so I couldn't tell if it was full. My flashlight made shadowy shapes on the grass. Something rustled in the bushes, and I swung my flashlight toward it. Caroline was watching me from the kitchen window, her hands cupped to keep out the light. I waved at her, zipped the tent closed, and turned on Jamie's flashlight.

I sat perfectly still on one of the sleeping bags, listening, but all I could hear were some crickets.

After a few minutes it didn't seem so scary. I picked up one of the comic books and opened the bag of marshmallows.

There was a sound, and something brushed against the side of the tent. "Meow."

"Daffy? Is that you?" I unzipped the tent door and let her in. She rubbed against me, purring. Mr. DeWitt always lets her out at night.

Suddenly Daffy arched her back and hissed. Outside the tent stood a shadowy figure. Then the zipper began to slide down.

"Martin, it's me," Caroline said, poking her head inside. "Can I sleep out here? It's hot in the house."

"Okay," I said. I never thought I'd be glad to see Caroline. "Want to play a game before we go to sleep?" I asked.

"Wait, and I'll play, too," Tim said. He zipped open the door and came in.

We set up a game in the middle of the floor and played until the flashlights began to flicker. Then we shut them off and tried to sleep.

"Martin?" Mom called from outside the tent door. "Robbie won't go to sleep. I thought you wouldn't mind if he slept with you." She climbed in, holding Robbie. She looked surprised to see Caroline and Tim.

"Robbie go tamping." He puckered up his lips and crawled into my sleeping bag.

"All right." I smiled. "But you have to go to sleep."

"Maybe I should just sleep here, too, in case he wakes up," Mom said. She took the blanket she'd brought and climbed on the other side of me, just as Dad stuck his head in the tent.

"I was afraid you might be lonely," he chuckled. "But instead I find my whole family out here. I guess I might as well join you."

I was squeezed in the middle, but it felt kind of good. Sometimes the middle is a good warm place to be. Robbie snuggled up close to me.

"Martin," he whispered sleepily. "Robbie wet pants."